CUMBRIA LIBRARIES

3 8003 04762 9662

FLYING

KKL

Cumbria
County Council

Libraries, books and more...........

KESWICK

- MAR 2019

1 0 MAR 2022

MARYPORT

- 6 NOV 2019

KT-491-486

Please return/renew this item by the last date shown.
Library items may also be renewed by phone on
030 33 33 1234 (24hours) or via our website

www.cumbria.gov.uk/libraries

Cumbria Libraries
CLIC
Interactive Catalogue

Ask for a CLIC password

PRESS

First published in Great Britain in 2016 by
Piccadilly Press
80-81 Wimpole Street, London, W1G 9RE
www.piccadillypress.co.uk

Text and illustrations copyright © Sir Chris Hoy, 2016

All rights reserved.
No part of this publication should be reproduced, stored or transmitted
in any form or by any means, electronic, mechanical, photocopying or
otherwise, without the written permission of the publisher.

The right of Sir Chris Hoy to be identified as author
of this work has been asserted by him in accordance
with the Copyright, Designs and Patents Act, 1988

This is a work of fiction. Names, places, events and incidents are either the
products of the author's imagination or are used fictitiously. Any resemblance to
actual persons, living or dead, or actual events, is purely coincidental.

A CIP catalogue record for this book is available from the British Library.

ISBN: 978-1-471-40524-2
also available as an ebook

1 3 5 7 9 10 8 6 4 2

Typeset in Berkeley Oldstyle
Printed and bound by Clays Ltd, St Ives PLC

Piccadilly Press is an imprint of Bonnier Zaffre,
a Bonnier Publishing Company
www.bonnierpublishingfiction.co.uk

Meet Fergus
and his friends...

Chimp

Fergus

Grandpa Herc

Mum

Daisy

Jambo Patterson

Calamity Coogan

Minnie McLeod

Belinda Bruce

Wesley Wallace

Dermot Eggs

Choppy Wallace

Mikey McLeod

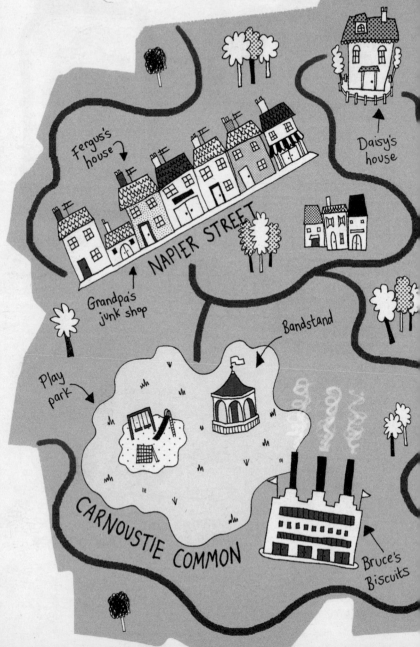

. . .and see where they live

Prince Waldorf

Dimmock

Knights of No Nonsense

King Woebegot

Hounds of Horribleness

Demelza

Meet Princess Lily
and her friends...

Princess Lily

Suet

Douglas

Unlucky Luke

Percy the Pretty Useless

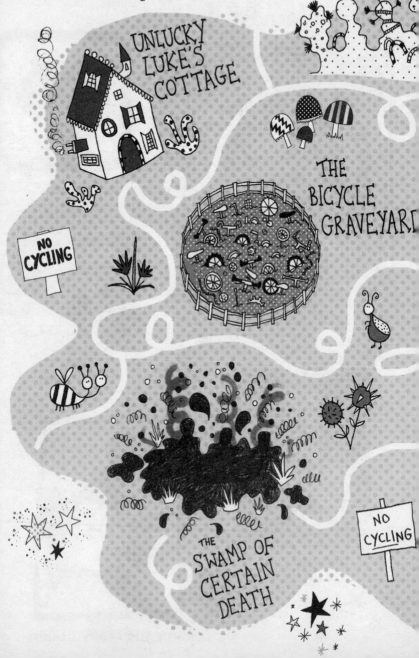

. . .and explore Nevermore

UNLUCKY LUKE'S COTTAGE

THE BICYCLE GRAVEYARD

NO CYCLING

NO CYCLING

THE SWAMP OF CERTAIN DEATH

Turret of Terror

Stables

Entrance to dungeon

Cook's pantry

Hounds of Horribleness Kennels

THE CASTLE

THE ENCHANTED FOREST

The Fancy Man

Fergus Hamilton was an ordinary nine-year-old boy. He liked athletics (but only on the telly), pizza (except when it had those small salty fish on it), and his dog Chimp (especially when he actually obeyed instructions like "sit", although that wasn't very often). He didn't like baths (but he had them), or times tables (but he learned them), or the way his mum sometimes put his socks in odd pairs (but he didn't change them back).

Yes, he was ordinary in almost every way, except one. Because, for a small boy, Fergus Hamilton had an extraordinarily big imagination.

Some days he imagined Chimp had just won the cup for Best In Show at the Annual All-Scotland Animal Extravaganza, instead of last place in the Waggiest Tail class in the local summer fair. (Chimp was having a sulk over not being allowed a sausage from the barbecue at the time.)

Some days he imagined he lived in a space camp on Pluto, fighting cosmic cowboys and discovering amazing aliens, instead of in the flat above his grandpa's second-hand bike shop on Napier Street.

But right now Fergus was imagining he was standing on the winners' podium at the District Championships, holding the golden trophy high above his head, his teammates Daisy, Calamity and Minnie at his side. He could hear the chorus of claps and cheers and smell the firework smoke from the party poppers being let off, but best of all was what he could see when he looked out into the crowd: Mum, Grandpa and Chimp, of course, but someone else too – a tall man with dark hair that stuck out in all the wrong directions and who had a familiar Hamilton smile.

His dad.

It was impossible, of course. Fergus's dad had disappeared nine years ago, and Fergus didn't even know what he looked like, not really, just a vague idea from a blurry old photo or two. Plus, Fergus had an inkling of an idea that his dad just *might* be in a parallel universe called Nevermore where he *could* have been transformed into a cantankerous kitchen cat called Suet, so chances were that he wasn't going to make the big race. But one thing about Fergus's dream was spot on: his cycle team the Hercules' Hopefuls really *did* have a shot at taking the prize. In the past few weeks they'd crunched seconds off their best lap times, and they would have crunched more if it hadn't been for the various bits and bobs that kept going wrong with their bikes.

"It's nothing that can't be fixed,"

said Grandpa, as Calamity looked sorrowfully at his spokes that had got bent for the third time in as many days, thanks to his habit of falling off as soon as he'd crossed the finish line.

"What about my saddle?" asked Daisy. "It keeps slipping until I'm so short my knees hit my nose when I cycle."

"And my brakes aren't tight enough," moaned Minnie.

"Nothing on my bike's tight enough," added Fergus. "I have to check it every night."

"And so you should," added Grandpa. "That's the problem when you get something brand new. You forget to check it and then WHAM BAM the chain slips and you hit the deck when you least expect it!"

"Maybe it's my chain that's the problem?" suggested the disaster-prone Calamity, who had a habit of hitting the deck. "Can you check it?"

"Maybe you can check him over while you're at it," giggled Minnie.

"Oh, very funny!" said Calamity, pretending it wasn't in the slightest bit amusing. But he couldn't resist a grin and soon the whole team was joking about the chances of him making it to the start line at the Districts without some kind of catastrophe.

Fergus laughed along with the others, but as he and Chimp wandered back along Napier Street towards home, he couldn't help glancing wistfully in the window of Wallace's Wheels at the new range of Sullivan Swifts that had just come in. Fergus had read all about them in his magazines: *Cycle News* said "the tech spec was top notch" – apparently these bikes were the lightest yet, with super-smooth gears and lightning-fast disc brakes. Best of all, each one had a distinctive decal sticker on the frame: flames for the Firebrand, an icicle for the Freezeframe and a lightning bolt for the Storm. Wesley, his arch-nemesis, was bound to have the Firebrand for the Districts – Wallace's Wheels was his dad's shop after all – and Fergus bet the rest of Wallace's Winners got a decent discount, too.

He sighed heavily. The District Championships were looming large over the team, and Fergus didn't hold out too much hope for their chances with their old bikes. The truth was that despite Grandpa's  optimism for make-do-and-mending, Fergus was a bit tired of his broken-down, second-hand life. "Even my family's wonky," he said to Chimp, as he propped his bike in the passageway and tightened the chain and saddle and brakes.

Chimp barked back, but it could have been "yes" or "I want a sausage" for all Fergus knew. So with no answers, just oily hands and a heavy heart, he headed upstairs for tea.

"Fergie!" exclaimed his mum. "Just in time. I've made your favourite!"

"Marmalade sandwiches?" Fergus said.

"Well, second favourite, then," admitted Mum, plopping fishfingers onto his plate. "Hurry up and sit down before they go cold."

"Don't you want me to wash my hands?" asked Fergus.

"Och, of course!" Mum laughed. "I wonder what's got into me?"

As Fergus soaped his hands in the sink, he wondered what had got into her too. Mum was never normally this chirpy before work. She was never normally this chirpy EVER!

"If you ask me," whispered Grandpa, as he reached over to get the ketchup, "she's got a fancy man!"

"A what?" asked Fergus, feeling his heart plummet horribly towards his tummy.

"A fella!" said Grandpa. "Haven't you noticed the new lipstick?"

Fergus hadn't, but then lipstick wasn't really high on his list of priorities.

Until now that is. Now that Grandpa had pointed it out, it seemed to be the most important thing in the world. All through tea he couldn't get the thought out of his head, until he just couldn't hold it in any more.

"Is – is that a new lipstick colour?" he asked.

Mum giggled. GIGGLED! "It is! Do you like it? It's called Vampire's Dream."

Fergus shuddered, but it wasn't the thought of bloodsuckers making him nervous, it was who his mum might be kissing with those lips. Fergus stood up quickly, his chair scraping on the floor.

"Don't you want your pudding?" Mum asked. "It's chocolate cake."

Fergus shook his head. "Lost my appetite," he said. "Can I go and lie down for a bit?"

Mum nodded. "Och, I hope you're not coming down with anything before the big race," she said, worriedly.

"He'll be fine," said Grandpa. "Just needs a wee break. And a think . . ." He gave Fergus a pointed look. "And then he'll realise everything's just fine. Fine and dandy."

But it wasn't fine. Or dandy.

"A fancy man," Fergus said to Chimp as he threw himself down on his bed.

"Of all the bad things that could happen – like summer holidays being banned, or cabbage being made compulsory or . . . or alien killer cats invading the world, THIS is way worse."

Chimp whimpered. Mrs MacCafferty's cat Carol was bad enough but alien ones? And killers, at that?

But Fergus didn't hear him. "If only I could get Dad back from Nevermore," he said. "Then everything would be all right. Then Mum wouldn't be looking twice at any men, fancy or otherwise."

Chimp howled, still thinking about alien cats.

"You said it, Chimp." Fergus sighed. "Fancy man," he repeated, and hid himself under the duvet where he stayed until morning.

The Stakeout

"A fancy man?" asked Daisy, after Fergus had snuck over to her house the next afternoon to report the bad news.

"That's what Grandpa reckons," said Fergus.

"But who?" asked Daisy.

"That's the worst bit," said Fergus. "I have no idea, and no way to find out either."

Daisy thought for a moment. "Right," she said. "It's easy."

"It is?" asked Fergus.

Daisy nodded. "We do what all superheroes do in this situation."

"Turn our watches into supersonic sonor detectors and then imprison the villains in a steel-spun spiderweb?" suggested Fergus, who had read a lot about superheroes in his comics.

"Er, I was thinking more we could make a list of possible suspects," said Daisy.

Fergus didn't think that sounded much like superhero activity to him, but it was a plan at least, and it was the only one they had. But after half an hour of thinking they had only come up with three possible names.

1. Mr Stewart, the school headmaster, who always said hello to Mum in the playground.

2. Rory Lomax's dad, Dougie, who once helped Mum pick up some tins of baked beans when she dropped them outside the corner shop.

3. Mr Nidgett, who ran the corner shop and had sold Mum the beans in the first place.

"But Mr Stewart is married to Mrs Stewart, which rules him out," said Daisy, crossing him off the list with a flourish.

"And Rory Lomax moved to East Kilbride three weeks ago," said Fergus, "so it can't be his dad either." (Which Fergus was rather glad about, because Rory ate paper, which Fergus thought was odd.)

"That leaves Mr Nidgett," said Daisy.

"But he's older than Grandpa!" protested Fergus. "And he's . . ." he struggled to remember how old Grandpa was " . . . ancient!"

"In that case, we'll have to put Plan B into action," announced Daisy.

"Plan B?" asked Fergus. "I didn't know we had one."

"You should always have a Plan B," said Daisy knowledgeably. "All the best superheroes know that."

Fergus was pretty sure his favourite superhero Captain Gadget didn't need a second go at anything but he didn't say that to Daisy. "So what is it then?" he asked.

"Stakeout!" cried Daisy, sending Chimp into a barking frenzy thinking he'd heard his second-favourite dinner being heralded.

"Ha!" laughed Daisy, ruffling Chimp's fur. "'Stake', not 'steak'. It means we follow your mum and find out what she's up to."

Which is exactly what they did.

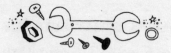

Tiptoeing as quietly as they could, and hiding behind lampposts when they needed to, Fergus, Daisy and Chimp followed Fergus's mum to Eat Your Peas Greengrocer's where she bought a bag of carrots and a cabbage.

"Oh, yuck!" said Fergus. "That's tea ruined."

Then they followed her to the Crumpets and Cream Café, where she met Mrs MacCafferty for a slice of Battenburg cake and a gossip about the traffic cones on Carnoustie Hill.

Last of all they followed her to the offices of the *Evening News* on Princess Street.

"What's she up to there?" asked Daisy, then gasped. "I've got it! The fancy man is Lester Sylvester!"

"The fat man who owns the newspaper and once got in trouble for making the news up on a boring day?"

"The very same!" insisted Daisy.

"Nah." Fergus shook his head. "She's just dropping in an advert for Grandpa's shop. I heard her offer to do it earlier."

"Oh, bother," said Daisy.

"With knobs on," added Fergus.

"Maybe there's no fancy man after all?" suggested Daisy.

Fergus felt the heaviness that had weighed down his insides for the last day or so lift slightly. "Maybe not," he agreed. "Maybe not!" After all, Grandpa wasn't always right about everything, was he? He grinned down at Chimp, who was bored and clearly sulking that he hadn't been allowed any Battenberg cake or even an old carrot. "Come on, boy. Time to go home, eh?"

"RUFF!" barked Chimp happily at the word 'home'.

"I agree," said Daisy.

And so, with a smile and a cheerful step, the trio set off back to Napier Street.

"So how much do you reckon we'll beat Wallace's lot by on Sunday?" asked Daisy.

"It's not just them, though, is it?" Fergus pointed out. "There's the Stirling Streaks to think about too."

"And the Falkirk Flyers," added Daisy grimly. "But I still think we've got a chance."

"Aye," he agreed. "More than a chance."

"We'll crush them!" cried Daisy.

"Annihilate them!" whooped Fergus.

"Make them eat dust!" Daisy danced around the pavement.

But Fergus wasn't dancing. Fergus wasn't even walking any more, because he'd seen something over the road. Something terrifying. Something that struck far more fear into him than the Falkirk Flyers ever could. Daisy saw it and stopped too.

"Oh, crikey," she said.

"My thoughts exactly," said Fergus.

Because there was his mum, talking to a man.

"Is that the . . ." began Daisy.

"Fancy man?" finished Fergus, barely managing to utter the words. Then he had a thought. "But he's married, isn't he?"

Daisy shook her head. "She ran off with a carpet fitter two Christmases ago. Everyone knows that. That's why all he cares about is winning."

"Until now," said Fergus, his stomach swirling and his legs feeling like jelly.

Because the man Mum was talking to, and smiling at, and even touching on the arm at one point, was none other than . . .

Choppy Wallace.

The Wicked Stepfather

Fergus sighed. And then he sighed again for good measure. The prospect of Choppy Wallace as a stepdad was weighing heavily on his mind. Not only had the distraction added three seconds to his track time that morning but, worse, it was putting him right off his marmalade sandwiches.

"You're worrying about the race, aren't you?" said Grandpa. "I can read you like a book."

Then you need glasses, thought Fergus. But he shrugged anyway. Best not to let on what he knew about Mum and Choppy Wallace.

"You've got to keep focused, Fergie," continued Grandpa. "Keep your eyes on the prize, remember?"

Fergus nodded. He remembered, of course he remembered. The problem was he *couldn't* keep focused because Choppy being his stepfather *did* matter. It mattered more than anything. He'd have to do what Choppy told him. He'd have to . . . OH NO! Fergus gulped. He'd just realized something even more humungously awful than Choppy being his stepdad . . .

Wesley would be his stepBROTHER!

So he'd have to put up with Wesley being rude to him *all* the time.

He'd have to share all his cycle magazines. Share his chocolate cake. Share his mum!

Besides, where would they fit? There was hardly room in the flat for him, Mum, Grandpa and Chimp, let alone Choppy and Wesley. Fergus shuddered at the thought.

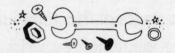

"Maybe you'll move into their house," suggested Daisy, who had popped round later that afternoon to borrow some bike mags. "That wouldn't be so bad. According to Wesley they've got a MAHOOSIVE garden and three tellies and a machine that makes fizzy drinks."

"And you think Wesley would let me watch *his* telly or drink *his* cola?" asked Fergus, though it wasn't really a question because he already knew the answer.

"Probably not," said Daisy. "But I've had a great idea – you can move in with me. That would be BEAST!"

Fergus smiled. At least there'd be no Wesley to deal with on a daily basis. But Daisy's house came with its own set of rules and regulations. Literally.

Pages and pages of them, laminated and stuck on the kitchen wall. They started off with:

1. Always wash your hands before eating.

2. No food in the front room or upstairs.

3. No touching anything with food on your hands.

And eventually moved on to:

44. No touching the candlesticks or the photo of Granny Devlin with the monkey.

45. No touching anything breakable.

46. No touching anything to see if it's breakable . . .

47. No even thinking about seeing what will flush down a toilet.

Worst of all was:

100. No dogs. Or dogs disguised as small children.

Daisy, of course, had tried all of them.

"Thanks, Dais," Fergus said. "But I couldn't abandon Chimp."

"What if we disguised him as a robot?" asked Daisy. "That's not against Mum's rules. Yet."

"He'd only eat the disguise," sighed Fergus, looking down at his mutt, who was busy chewing a pair of pants. Besides, he thought, what about Mum and Grandpa? He'd need to stick close to them in case Choppy was planning something super-evil, like dangling them over a pool of starving piranhas, or trapping them in his underground lair in a disused volcano, both of which had nearly happened to Captain Gadget in the last two copies of his comic.

Just as Fergus was imagining a close-up on Choppy's face laughing maniacally as he winched them lower over the snapping water, the doorbell rang, making him jump and Chimp yelp.

"Crikey," said Daisy, "keep your wig on, it's the door not a thunderclap."

"Sorry," said Fergus. "Daydreaming again. It's probably Mr Munt from number 32 come to fix the washing machine."

But when Fergus, Daisy and Chimp trooped out to the hall to see who it was they were in for another shock.

Because it wasn't Mr Munt from number 32 come to fix the washing machine.

And it wasn't Mrs MacCafferty from two doors down come to borrow some sugar.

And it wasn't Mrs Flynn from two doors up come to borrow some flour.

It was Fergus's worst nightmare, disguised as an ordinary man in a baseball cap.

It was Choppy Wallace.

"Choppy, what a surprise!" Fergus's mum smiled.

Fergus didn't.

"What can we do you for?" asked Grandpa, who wasn't smiling either.

"Nice to see you, Mrs Hamilton, Herc." Choppy nodded to them. "I've got a proposal for you."

A proposal! Fergus gulped and glanced at Daisy, whose eyes were practically popping out.

"Or rather an offer, if you like."

Daisy's eyes popped a little less, but Fergus still nudged her nervously. "What if it's . . .?"

"What if it's what?" asked Grandpa. "Will someone tell me what's going on?"

Choppy laughed. "Of course. It's . . ."

Fergus and Daisy held their breath.

" . . . bikes, of course."

"Huh?" said Fergus and Daisy together.

"You heard," said Choppy. "I want to offer Hercules' Hopefuls four Sullivan Swifts, free of charge, for the Districts."

In books people always pinched themselves when someone said something unbelievable so Fergus tried it, but all that happened was that he got a sore bit on his arm and Choppy was still there claiming to be offering him and the rest of his team free bikes. Free Sullivan Swifts!

"Top of the range, mind," Choppy added. "Firebrands or Freezeframes, you choose."

"It's a trap," said Daisy, who was as suspicious of Choppy as Fergus was.

"Hey, hey," said Grandpa. "That's enough." But then he turned to Choppy. "What's in it for you?" Grandpa asked.

"The Districts are at Middlebank. That's Wallace's Winners' home track, which gives us an unfair advantage. Just trying to even it out."

"Oh, come on!" exclaimed Grandpa. "You're a canny businessman, it can't be just for the love of the race."

Choppy smiled. *Like a crocodile*, Fergus thought to himself.

"You're fairly canny yourself, Herc," said Choppy. "Okay, I'll admit it: advertising. I'm the only supplier of Sullivan Swifts in the city. It'll get more people into my shop if two teams are racing my bikes."

"Aye, and fewer into mine," said Grandpa.

"Maybe," said Choppy. "But isn't giving your team the best chance of winning more important? Besides, can't let those Falkirk Flyers beat us in our home city, eh?"

"He's right," said Mum before Grandpa could even think of a reply. "It's a marvellous offer. Of course the answer is 'yes'."

Fergus looked at Grandpa.

Grandpa looked at Fergus and shrugged. "When your mam's mind's made up, it's made up," he said. "What do you say?"

"I say no way, José," said Daisy. "It's a big scam."

"Och, you don't know that," said Grandpa. "Give the man a chance. Fergie?"

Fergus felt himself being pulled every which way. He'd just been offered what he'd always wanted – a brand new bike, a Sullivan Swift, no less, the bike of his dreams – but by his worst enemy. Unless . . . maybe he'd got it all wrong. Maybe Choppy wasn't as bad as all that. Mum seemed to like him after all. And even though Mum had told Fergus that one day he'd like broccoli, and that hadn't come true yet, she was right about most other things.

Maybe he just needed to give Choppy a chance. That's what Grandpa said. After all, he'd said the same about Calamity and Minnie, and look how well they'd worked out. Yes, that was it. He was going to do the right thing, and give Choppy Wallace the benefit of the doubt. And bag himself a brilliotic bike in the process!

"Aye," he said, finally. "Thanks, Choppy. That'd be great."

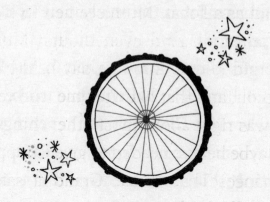

Sabotage!

"I still think it's a trick," said Daisy, as the team wheeled their Sullivan Swifts to the starting line at the cinder track on Carnoustie Common.

"I don't see how," said Calamity, admiring the flame decal on his Firebrand, and trying not to trip over the pedals. "We get brand new bikes and a better chance of winning. What's not to like?"

"Exactly," agreed Minnie, running

her fingers down the steely blue of her Freezeframe.

Fergus didn't know what to think. Part of him believed this had to be a trick, because Choppy hadn't ever done the decent thing before, let alone an amazing thing. At the tryout for his team he'd even encouraged Wesley to drop his bike in Fergus's way so Fergus muffed the race.

But Calamity was right, they had new bikes, and what wasn't beast about that? Maybe Choppy really did have a heart somewhere in there after all. Mum obviously thought so. Fergus felt his stomach swirl and quickly pushed that thought away again. "Eyes on the prize," he said to himself. Then to his team, "Right, one lap it is, and remember we're just getting used to the bikes, not trying to beat each other."

"Got it," said Daisy.

"Roger," agreed Calamity.

"What they said," echoed Minnie.

"On your marks . . ." began Fergus, and poised his own foot on his right pedal ready to push down, " . . . get set . . . GO!"

Fergus felt the wind whip his face as he set off along the cinder track. *Woah!* he thought, surprised by how slick his start had been. In fact, the Firebrand was everything the advertisements claimed it would be: "speedy, smooth and light as a feather". "Swift" really was the word. Fergus careered around the far corners, Daisy and Minnie level-pegging behind him, Calamity bringing up the rear. *There was no denying it*, Fergus thought, *this was one incredible bike. Except that something . . .* Fergus frowned. Something wasn't quite right.

Fergus thought and thought as he tried to put his finger on just what it was that was wrong. The brakes were tight and responsive; the wheels spun along the track like a knife through hot butter; the frame was the perfect design, forcing him long and low over the crossbar.

There was nothing specific he could blame. But as he headed up the home straight, he slowly realised what the problem was. He hadn't got that feeling – that feeling like the very first time he had ridden his old, second-hand bike – that he was about to take flight, that there was nothing at that moment in time that he couldn't do.

Instead, as he flew across the finishing line, Fergus just felt blank.

He pulled hard on the brakes and pulled the bike to a neat stop; his teammates doing the same just seconds later. Well, except Calamity, who seemed to prefer his usual method of crashing into a bush.

"That. Was. BEAST!" exclaimed Daisy.

"Unbe-LEIV-able!" agreed Minnie.

"Grrrgglmmpphh!" said Calamity with a mouthful of leaves, but the smile on his face was clear, even if his words weren't.

"Yeah," said Fergus. "Brilliotic."

But it wasn't. It was just that everyone else seemed so enthusiastic he didn't want to spoil the mood.

"Maybe it's because it's my first go," he said to Chimp as he wheeled his Firebrand back down Napier Street after practice. "It'll get better, I'm sure."

But it didn't. Every day Fergus took the bike out before school and afterwards. And every day he cut a fraction of a second off his lap-time. But he still didn't get that electric feeling, where your tummy whizzes and your brain fizzes and you think your whole body might just launch into outer space.

All he felt was fast.

And there was another thing. What if this bike didn't have that other kind of magic? The kind that let him take off and fly from this world to Nevermore. "I'm going to have to give it a go," he said to himself. "Right here and right now."

So he did. He got the bike up to full speed, then did what he'd always done, closed his eyes and let the pedals spin back once, twice, three times. Then . . .

Nothing.

When he opened his eyes he was still very much on Carnoustie Common, just going a bit slower and heading straight for the bandstand. Fergus pushed down on the pedals and pulled hard on the brakes trying to regain control, and that's when it happened.

CLUNK!

CRACK!

CRASH!

The front wheel sailed right off the frame of the Firebrand, and Fergus sailed straight into the side of the bandstand.

"Ow!" he said as he picked himself and the bike up off the ground. "Ow, ow, OW!"

Nothing was broken, though. Nothing on Fergus, at least. But the bike was another story.

"Faulty part," he moaned to Chimp, as he limped slowly home, the wheel in one hand and the frame over his shoulder. "Must be."

When he went to inspect the damage, Grandpa was in agreement.

"They churn these bikes out," he said. "Only stands to reason some of them are going to have faults and foibles."

Daisy peered at the wheel. "If you ask me, that's no fault, that's sabotage."

"Sabotage?" Fergus felt his heart flip.

"Look," she said. "See where someone's sliced right through that part?"

Fergus looked. It did seem neat and sharp, almost too neat and sharp to have just sheared.

"The question is," Daisy went on, "who would have done it?"

Fergus's heart and stomach sank. Because there was only one person it *could* be: Choppy Wallace. Daisy had known it all along. Fergus had just hoped for better because he'd finally got his hands on the cycle of his dreams. *Some dream*, he thought, as he looked at his bruised knees and broken bike.

"Hey, hey!" Grandpa interrupted his thoughts, and Daisy who was about to add to her theory. "Sabotage is a big thing to go accusing anyone of. We don't know that the bike was tampered with for sure. Point is, it's happened now,

49

so all we can do is fix it. Until then, you'll have to train on your old bike."

Fergus sighed. This was going from bad to worse. The Districts were almost upon them, his brand new Sullivan Swift was out of action, and to make matters worse, he was pretty sure his Mum was making eyes at the champion cheat himself.

Nothing could fix this. Not even Grandpa.

Unless . . .

Fergus had a thought. If he could just get his dad back, then maybe, just maybe, he could at least stop the whole fancy man business in its tracks, even if the race was lost.

"About my old bike," piped up Fergus. "I reckon I'll take it for a spin right now."

"Now?" asked Grandpa. "But it's

almost teatime. And your mam's going out in an hour."

"I'll be back by tea," Fergus promised. "There's just a little something I have to do first."

And I have to do it now, he said to himself. I have to get to Nevermore and track down that cat, find out if it really is Dad. And if it IS, then I need to turn him back into human form. Then I have to somehow get him back here before Mum goes out on her date with Choppy so she can fall in love with Dad again. So he left Daisy and Grandpa gazing at the broken Firebrand and headed out again on his old bike.

"Easy-peasy," he said to Chimp as they hurried back to the Common. "Easy-peasy, lemon-squeezy."

But it wasn't easy or peasy, and Fergus knew it. And even though he was setting off on his trusty old bike with his friend at his side, he had never felt more frightened in his life.

Percy the Pretty Useless

Fergus had one thing worked out, at least. Wherever in Nevermore he thought of while he was backpedalling, that's where he would land. So this time, when his bike touched down, he headed straight for the home of Unlucky Luke. Yes, there was the danger of ending up as an experiment for Luke's dad, but even though Percy the Pretty Useless was the world's worst court magician, he was also Fergus's only hope.

"Jeepers, mate!" exclaimed Chimp when they pulled up outside the hut. "What is that stink?"

Fergus sniffed, then wished he hadn't. It was as if someone had got a bottle of gone-off milk, tipped it over some very old socks then worn them to tread in dog poo.

"Ewww," he complained. "Where is that coming from?"

Fergus didn't have to wait long to find out, because at that very moment

the door burst open and Unlucky Luke burst out, closely followed by a short man in a spangly cloak and slightly on-fire hat, which he put out by sticking his entire head in a water trough.

"That's better," sighed the man, his soggy hat smouldering. "Next time I'll add a little less foot of frog."

"And a lot less cheese," added Luke, before turning to see his friends. "Fergus! Chimp! Good to see you! This is my dad, Percy."

Percy nodded at the pair, who nodded slowly back.

"Fergus?" came another voice from inside the hut. A sooty face appeared, followed by an even sootier body, dressed in boys' breeches, and a curly-haired head topped with a tiara.

"Lily!" Fergus exclaimed, going to hug the princess, then thinking better of it and high-fiving her instead.

"Just in time," said Lily. "Cook's on the warpath over the mess we made in the kitchen, plus Waldorf blabbed about the bicycle so Dad's on the warpath over that! You have to do something, Fergus!"

"I will," he promised. "At least, I'll try. But I have to fix something first."

"About that," said Lily. "Me and Luke, we worked it out."

Luke nodded. "You see, your dad disappeared nine years ago. Which is exactly when . . ."

" . . . Suet showed up," said Fergus, feeling hope bubble up inside him like sodapop.

"And," continued Lily, "Percy specialises in turning people into . . ."

"Animals!" finished Fergus.

Luke grinned. "Which would mean that . . ."

57

Fergus gulped. "My dad is . . ."

"Suet the cat!" chorused the threesome.

"You've got to be kidding me," said Chimp, who was the only one not excited by this prospect.

"Not at all," said Percy. He was still managing to emit a slight essence of "ick". "You're all spot on. I'm just sorry you didn't work it out sooner."

"You could have fessed up, Dad," Luke scolded. "You knew exactly what you'd done, after all."

"Hang on, you did it on purpose?" demanded Fergus.

"I'm sorry," said the magician, "but what else was I supposed to do? King Woebegot ordered me to shrink him until he disappeared for good. At least this way your dad is still alive."

"But turning him into a cat?" said Chimp, disgusted.

"They live longer than dogs," said Luke.

"Plus they get nine lives," said Lily, "which is lucky, living with Cook."

"Well, where's Suet now?" asked Fergus. "What if he's lost another life while we've been standing around talking?"

"No chance." Lily smiled. "I tracked him down to the stables this morning and shut him in a cardboard box."

"A box?" asked Fergus, worriedly. "Will he be okay?"

"Course," said Lily.

"All cats love boxes," added Luke.

"Shame we can't keep 'em all shut up," muttered Chimp, thinking of Mrs MacCafferty's cat Carol.

"It's one thing catching him," said Fergus. "But another actually changing him back into a human."

"We need an antidote," said Chimp.

Fergus gave him an incredulous look.

"What? You think I can't read Captain Gadget comics, too?" asked the dog.

Fergus didn't know what to think, but he didn't have time to even think about that, because he was interrupted by Percy shoving a single small bottle into his hand.

"What's this?" he asked.

"Possible antidote," said Percy. "But be careful. It's strong. And, also . . . largely untested."

"Untested?" protested Chimp. "Now come on, mate, you can't be expecting us to use some kind of poison on our lad's daddy now."

"I'm sorry," said Percy, "but the ingredients are . . . unusual and rare, and there's not much of it. I didn't want to waste it."

"If it works, can we use it on me?" asked Luke. "I'd like to finally get rid of these chicken feet and bear paws."

"If you remember to save some," said Percy. "And don't get turned into monkeys in the process."

"MONKEYS?" wailed Chimp. "Now he tells us."

But Fergus ignored him. He didn't care about the chance of turning into a chimp – an actual chimp, that is – all he cared about was his dad. "Come on, boy," he said. "Buck up. Time to put Operation Catnap into practice."

"Operation Catnap!" repeated Lily, swinging her leg over her own bicycle.

"Too right!" agreed Luke, hopping on for a backie.

Fergus pulled his own bike up from the floor. "Operation Catnap," he said again, quieter this time. "This had better work."

And with a still-grumbling Chimp stuck on the handlebars, and Percy's "Good luck" echoing in his ears, he set off to find a cantankerous cat and turn him into the father he had never met.

The Antidote

Cats may well love sleeping in cardboard boxes, but being shut in them, even with snacks, toys and several air holes, is another thing entirely. So by the time Fergus and friends arrived at the stable, Suet was in the foulest of tempers.

"Here, kitty, kitty," called Fergus through the air holes.

"Dad, you mean," said Chimp, matter-of-factly.

"True," admitted Fergus. And, although it felt weird to say it, he did it anyway, calling, "Here, Dad – I mean Hector – I mean . . . Oh, I don't know what I mean. He probably doesn't understand anyway."

"That's what you think," said Chimp, improbably raising a hairy eyebrow. "We animals understand everything. EVERYTHING, I tell you."

Fergus knelt down and carefully opened the lid.

"Hey, Dad," he said. "It's me, Fergus. Don't be frightened."

But, for once, Chimp seemed to be wrong, because instead of calmly listening, Suet let out a terrible *YOOOOOOOOWWWWWWWWWLLL* and tried to make a bolt for it back towards the kitchen.

"Not a chance," declared Lily, grabbing

Suet around the middle and wrestling the cat to the floor.

"Ha!" laughed a voice from the shadows. "A cat's about all you *could* tackle."

Fergus flicked his head round and saw, to his horror, the figure of Lily's twin brother emerge from a haystack, followed by his dimwitted sidekick.

"Shut it, Waldorf," snapped Lily. "This is none of your business."

"Oh, but it is," said Waldorf. "Think of the presents I'll get when I tell Daddy you've got that boy racer here again, and his stinking hound." He gave Chimp a filthy look, who gave him an even filthier one back. "Besides, you're already in trouble as it is."

"Yeah, trouble," repeated Dimmock.

"You wouldn't," dared Lily.

"Would too."

"Would not."

"Would too."

"Would not."

"Whatever," said Waldorf eventually, and thankfully, because Fergus was worried Lily couldn't hold Suet for much longer as well as argue.

"Where are you going?" demanded Lily, as her brother and his shadow slunk towards the door.

"Where do you think?" replied Waldorf, smiling over his shoulder, before slamming the door.

"The king," said Luke.

Lily nodded. "He's gone to fetch Dad. So we'd better get a shimmy on. Where's the antidote?"

Fergus didn't need to be asked twice and pulled the bottle out of his pocket.

"It's probably useless," said Luke gloomily. "I'm still waiting for my claws to be turned back to feet – none of Dad's other potions have worked. And turning a cat into a human is way more difficult."

"Oh, piffle," said Lily. "Let's be positive."

Fergus nodded. That's what Grandpa was always telling him. Always hope for the best and you might just get your wish. He uncorked the bottle.

Which was the exact moment Suet managed to dig his claws into Lily, who let out a yell, which made Suet let out a caterwaul and shoot straight up a beam into the rafters.

"Well, that's torn it," said Chimp. "Flaming cats. Not to be trusted, I tell you."

"I'm sorry," Lily apologised.

"Don't worry," said Luke. "One of us needs to climb up, that's all."

"That's all?" exclaimed Fergus.

Luke nodded. "But not me, with these things." He looked down at his bear paws and chicken claws.

"Me neither!" declared Chimp. "I don't do heights. Or cats. Or those funny pink wafer biscuits. But mainly heights. And cats."

"I'll go," said Lily.

"No, I'll go," said Fergus. "He's my dad. Or at least, I think he is. It should be me. Besides, I've climbed hundreds of trees. How hard can it be?"

Quite hard, as it turns out. It was a long way up.

Fergus shimmied up a post, the potion safe in his pocket, and managed to clamber onto the main beam. But crawling along it was a different matter.

For a start, his eyes were no longer looking at the roof. Now when he looked down he felt his stomach swirl. It was okay, somehow, when he was flying through the air to get to Nevermore. But on his own, without his faithful bike, and without that magic, he felt horribly scared being so high up.

"Focus, Fergie!" cried Chimp.

"Forget about us!" yelled Lily.

Easier said than done, thought Fergus. But slowly, steadily, he inched forward, trying not to scare Suet, until he was just close enough.

"Here we go, Hector," he said, staring into the cat's wide, bright eyes.

"*Hissss*," replied the frightened feline.

Too scared to let go completely, Fergus uncorked the bottle with his teeth, then quick as a wink flung the liquid at the cat.

There was crash, a whoosh, a smell of burnt leather and baby powder, and then, to Fergus's absolute astonishment, what perched before him on the beam was not an angry kitchen cat, but a man. A fully-grown man, wearing cycle kit. With dark hair that stuck out in every direction. And what's more, with a very familiar face.

"Dad?" asked Fergus, feeling himself shiver with excitement.

"Fergus?" asked the man.

But before Fergus could reply, the doors burst open below them and a gust of wind swept through the stable.

"Woah!" yelled Fergus, wobbling wildly.

"Waah!" yelled the man, swaying from side to side.

They instinctively grabbed onto each other, then, with one almighty swing, tipped over the beam and fell through the air before landing on their backs on a haystack.

"Bonzer!" cried Chimp, bounding over to his master.

Fergus opened his eyes. Then blinked to make sure he really was alive, and this really was who he thought it was, smiling in front of him.

"My-my n-name's Fergus," he stammered. "Fergus Hamilton. Are you – ?"

The man opened his mouth to speak but another voice answered.

"Hector Hamilton," it said. "We meet again."

Fergus jumped to his feet to see not just Prince Waldorf this time, but a taller, grouchier-looking version of him. This must be . . .

"King Woebegot," said Hector.

"The very same," the king replied. "The king who sentenced you to shrinkage nine years ago, and the king who is arresting you now for disobedience. And that pesky Percy too, once my Knights of No Nonsense get their hands on him."

The Knights of No Nonsense nodded furiously in agreement.

"And he scratched my hands four times when he was a cat," added Waldorf. "Don't forget that."

"Yes, you can add that to the charge list," King Woebegot said to the chief knight, who wrote it down on an important-looking pad of paper.

"You can't arrest my dad!" cried Fergus. "I've only just got him back."

"He can," hissed Lily. "And he is. And he'll arrest you too, if you don't disappear sharpish."

"No way!" said Fergus. "I won't leave. He's my dad. I've only just found him."

"Trust me," said Lily, lowering her voice. "I can handle things here. All you need to do is come back at almost exactly the same time you left.

And with a plan. That way nothing bad . . . well, nothing REALLY bad will have happened yet. But right now, you're in danger of being arrested too and then we're all in serious trouble. If you've got half a brain you'll do as I say and RUN!"

Fergus looked at his dad.

But his dad was on Lily's side, and nodded. "It's okay," Hector whispered. "I can look after myself. But you need to go. Now!"

So Fergus did what his dad told him. With Chimp at his heels, he charged for the side door, jumped on his bike and pedalled as hard as he could.

"After them!" yelled Wesley.

"After them!" yelled the king.

"After them!" yelled the chief knight.

"After them!" yelled the rest of the Knights of No Nonsense. Until they realized that they were the ones who were supposed to be doing the "after them" bit, so they jumped on their hover bikes and headed after Fergus and Chimp.

★

"What's that noise?" whimpered Chimp as the pair flew through the forest on Fergus's bike.

"The Hounds of Horribleness," admitted Fergus, breathlessly.

"Not again!" wailed Chimp. "They sound . . . horrible!"

The barking behind was beginning to close in.

Fergus leaned forward, flat as he could over the handlebars. "We'll be fine," he promised. "Trust me." Then he closed his eyes, let his feet slip backwards three times, and hoped harder than ever that the magic still worked . . .

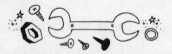

WHOMP! Fergus and Chimp landed back on Carnoustie Common, their hearts racing, and Fergus's legs tingling with exhaustion.

But at least they were safe. For now. And, if Fergus did what Lily had asked, his dad would be too.

Fergus grinned to himself. With Chimp panting along beside him, he carried on grinning all the way across the common, right along Napier Street and into the passageway where he parked his bike.

"I don't see what you're smiling about," said Grandpa, looking up from the wreck of Fergus's Sullivan Swift.

"Because I've realized something," said Fergus.

"Och aye?" said Grandpa. "That we've got two days until Districts and the whole team's bikes are broken – Daisy and Minnie and Calamity's Swifts are riddled with faults too – and I can't get my hands on the right bicycle parts for at least a week?"

"Nope," said Fergus. "Anyway, we won't be needing parts. We won't be needing the Swifts at all."

"And why's that?" asked Grandpa.

"Because the magic isn't in fancy new wheels," said Fergus. "It's in us. And I don't feel it on the Firebrand, only on my birthday bike."

"What are you saying?" asked Grandpa.

"I'm saying I want to ride my old bike in the Districts. I'm saying the whole team should."

Grandpa stood up, stretched his aching shoulders, and smiled. "You sound like someone else I know," he said. "Or once knew. Good on you, laddie. I'll get cracking on the oiling and tuning of our own bikes first thing in the morning. But right now, I think we should both get ourselves some rest."

Fergus nodded. A rest was just what he needed. And a long one at that.

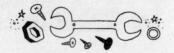

That night, as he lay under the covers, waiting for sleep to take him, Fergus allowed himself a last grin. Magic. That was what it felt like – riding in Nevermore, and here too. Even when he was just flying across the grass or cinder track instead of in the air.

And if he could just hold on to that magic feeling, then maybe, just maybe, they had a chance of beating Wallace's Winners.

With that glimmer of hope in his heart, Fergus finally fell fast asleep.

To Cheat or Not To Cheat?

But that glimmer of hope faded fast the next day when Fergus's mum had been giggling on the phone for half an hour, and when Fergus asked who it was, she said it was "none of his beeswax".

The night before she'd disappeared out on a date to Dancing Dave's Disco. She wouldn't say who with, but Fergus was pretty sure it was not Mrs MacCafferty, who had two left feet and a gyppy hip.

And now, as the team gathered at Middlebank for the Districts, Fergus felt his bad luck was on a roll.

"We're doomed," Fergus said to Daisy despondently. "Mum's going to marry Choppy Wallace and we're going to lose the race. To my *stepbrother*." He flicked a sulky look over at Wesley, who flicked a sneery one back.

"At least we know our bikes won't break halfway round," said Minnie.

"I still don't believe anyone would do that," said Grandpa, looking up from a final tune-up.

"I do," said Daisy, eyeing up Wesley and the rest of Wallace's Winners as they smoothed down their silk jerseys and checked the saddles on their own Sullivan Swifts. "Even if it wasn't Choppy's lot it could be one of the other teams. I've never liked the look of Lacey Lewington."

"Only because she once beat you in the sack race at the summer fair," said Fergus.

"She bagsied the biggest sack." Daisy scowled. "Easier to handle."

"What about the Falkirk Flyers?" asked Calamity. "I heard their number three Manjit Green once ate four cans of baked beans before a race for extra jet propulsion."

Minnie giggled and Daisy pulled a face. "Gross!" she said.

But Fergus knew it wasn't Manjit or Lacey or any of the riders on their teams. He was convinced there was only one possible culprit, and he was staring right at them with his usual smirk.

"Couldn't take the pace on the Swifts, then?" teased Wesley.

"Back to your old bangers!" added Belinda Bruce, their number four.

"Yeah, bangers," echoed Dermot Eggs.

"Never mind, little sis," said Mikey McLeod. "Maybe next year you'll have something less . . . old." He looked straight at Grandpa.

Grandpa bristled. "I . . . these bikes may be old, but they're better tuned than anything you lot are riding. I checked them myself." And he had. Grandpa had spent hours going over them all with a fine-toothed comb, or rather a spanner and a can of oil. "Out of date doesn't mean out of action," he'd said as he twiddled and fiddled and finally gave them all a polish.

At the time, Fergus had agreed with him, but right now, on the starting line of their most important race so far, he wasn't so sure they could pull it off. "We're out of practice on these though," he said.

"It's true," agreed Minnie. "We're used to Swifts now."

"Muscle memory," said Grandpa, knowledgeably. "The minute you get out there, your legs and arms will mould themselves back into the right shape for the bikes. Mark my words."

Fergus shrugged.

"I still think we should have sabotaged their bikes right back," said Daisy.

"Aye," said Calamity. "Slashed their tyres."

"And buckled their wheels," added Minnie.

Grandpa shook his head. "If there's one thing that Hercules' Hopefuls are not it's cheaters," he insisted. "If we win this, we'll win it fair and square. Deal?"

Fergus and his teammates looked at each other, smiles slowly spreading across their faces. "Deal!" they chorused.

"Good on you, kids." Grandpa grinned at them. "Now, saddle up, we've only seconds to go!"

Middlebank Mayhem

Fergus surveyed the scene for one final time as he settled into his starting position. The crowd was massive, much bigger than any he'd ridden in front of before. Amongst them he could just pick out familiar faces: Mum, Mrs MacCafferty, Daisy's mum Mrs D, even good old James "Jambo" Patterson from the *Evening News*. Despite his nickname being the same as the local football team, Jambo was a cycling fan through and through. But the other teams had hordes of supporters too, some with placards and banners, some with rattles, and all cheering the names of their favourites.

"Go Flyers!" he heard.

"Come on you Streaks!" shouted another voice. "Give 'em what for!"

Then, "Wallop them, Winners! You know what to do!"

Fergus glanced over to where that shout had come from and saw Choppy Wallace himself, staring steadily back at him.

"Yeah?" Fergus said to himself. "Well, I know what to do, too." And, newly determined, he lowered himself over the handlebars and waited for the countdown.

"On your marks!" cried the umpire. "Get set . . . GO!"

Fergus went, flying along the smooth, hard tarmac of the track with ease. Grandpa was right, it didn't feel strange at all, it felt easy. In fact, it felt perfect.

One day, when he grew taller and his legs grew longer, Fergus knew he'd need a new bike. But right now, this was the only one he wanted: the bike built by his grandpa with old bits and bobs, but more importantly, with love and care – the best bike he could wish for.

"Go for it, Fergie!" Jambo yelled as Fergus passed him.

"Yes, come on!" Mum joined in.

Fergus kept his focus, but let himself feel a smidgen of satisfaction as he powered ahead. *Things feel right when I'm riding*, he thought to himself. Never mind Mum's fancy man, never mind Dad being stuck in a prison cell in a parallel universe – right here, right now he felt good. What's more, he was snug in Calamity's slipstream, enjoying an easy ride, saving power for the final push. He glanced to his right and caught a wink from Daisy who was doing the same behind Minnie.

And they'd need that push for sure, because although they were way ahead of the Stirling Streaks, both Wallace's Winners and the Falkirk Flyers were way out in front, the Flyers a bike length ahead of the Winners apiece as they rounded the far bend and started up the home straight. They didn't have a hope of catching up with the Falkirk lot but with a bit of hard work and luck they might just make some ground on Wesley and his gang. Fergus pushed harder and harder on the pedals, Grandpa's voice ringing in his head: "Just when you think you can't give it any more, that's when you need to dig deep and pull the old rabbit out of the hat."

Well, Fergus didn't have a rabbit, but he did have grit and determination – not just to do well for his team's sake, but to show Wesley and Choppy that cheating was for losers. "Come on," he urged himself. "You can do it!"

No sooner had he said those words than Calamity and Minnie played out what they'd been taught in practice, easing off the pedals slightly and moving to the side to let their team's numbers one and two through. Fergus felt himself surge forward, passing Belinda Bruce the biscuit heiress, as well as dimwitted Dermot Eggs. That left only Minnie's big brother Mikey and Wesley himself.

"I can't make it," he heard Daisy pant. "It's too much."

"You can!" he managed to reply, the words almost sticking in his throat. "Give it a shot. Your best one."

He saw Daisy grit her teeth and drop her head a fraction of an inch; he did the same, making himself more streamlined. Then, side by side, the pals pushed down and down on the pedals in perfect time as they flew towards the finish line.

But as they crossed the white chalk tape marking the end of the race, they both knew that their best hadn't been quite good enough. They were placed third, behind Wallace's Winners in second and the Falkirk Flyers in first.

Fergus and Daisy pulled off their helmets and dropped with their bikes to the floor, Minnie and Calamity following suit just seconds later.

"Well, that's that then," said Daisy sulkily, when they'd got their breath back. "No Nationals for us."

"Unless they decide to take the top three not just the top two," said Minnie, hopefully, remembering how they qualified for the Districts.

"No chance," said Calamity. "No one gets that lucky a second time. It's like lightning never striking twice. Which is a relief for me."

Fergus just sighed and stole a look at Wesley, who was arguing with Mikey about who got to hold the runner's up trophy. And as for the Falkirk Flyers, they all seemed to be shouting at each other, as well as at their coach and two of the officials. *Eedjits*, Fergus thought to himself. If Hercules' Hopefuls had got a trophy the whole team would have shared the prize and no one would be moaning.

"Great effort," said Grandpa, who'd managed to fight his way through the crowd.

"Aye!" said Mum, just steps behind him. "You really showed them."

"Showed them what?" demanded Fergus despondently. "How to be a loser? What about proving that cheating doesn't pay?"

"Now, come on," urged Grandpa. "You didn't lose, you were third – that's a bronze medal in my book."

"Shame your book isn't actually real," muttered Fergus.

"What IS going on over there?" asked Daisy, nodding at the Flyers, who were shouting even louder than ever, and now had a crowd gathered round them including all the race officials and Jambo Patterson, who was waving a microphone.

"Not a clue," admitted Grandpa.

"Maybe it's about who's got the best bike," suggested Minnie.

"Not any of us," said Daisy. "If only we'd had those Swifts, we could have beaten them."

"Oh, I don't know," said Fergus. Because even though he hadn't managed to match his lap time on the Sullivan Swift, it had definitely felt good to be back where he belonged.

But Fergus was shaken from his quiet contemplation by Minnie nudging him.

"Look," she said quietly.

Fergus looked up to see Jambo charging towards them, a massive grin on his face.

"You're not going to believe it, Jeanie," he said.

"Believe what?" asked Mum.

"Yeah, believe what?" said Daisy and Fergus together.

Jambo turned to the team. "The Falkirk Flyers have only gone and got themselves disqualified!"

Fergus felt his heart give a little leap. "Disqualified?" he blurted.

"They used illegal extensions on the handlebars," Jambo confirmed. "So they'd get lower down with less resistance and go faster."

"Does this mean . . .?" began Grandpa.

"Yes!" answered Jambo.

"Mean what?" demanded Fergus, almost bursting with hope.

"It means," said Grandpa, "that you're in second place after all."

Fergus felt happiness soak through him like butter on a hot crumpet, then the familiar feel of Daisy's arms flung around him. "We did it, Fergie!" she cried. "We really did it!"

"We did." Fergus smiled. "We really did."

"And without cheating," added Grandpa.

"Shame we can't get Choppy's lot disqualified," said Calamity.

"For what?" asked Jambo, sticking the voice recorder under Calamity's nose.

Grandpa yanked it away. "Nothing," he said. "Well, nothing that we can prove. Look, keep that off the record, please, Jambo – I don't want anyone thinking the Hopefuls are sore losers. Besides, we've got another chance to prove ourselves properly in two months' time."

"At the Nationals?" checked Fergus.

Grandpa nodded. "At the Nationals."

Date Night

Grandpa made tea again that night – meat pie and potatoes. But even though it was Fergus's third favourite dinner, and even though they were allowed to eat it on their laps in front of the telly, and even though they had jelly AND ice cream for pudding, Fergus still hadn't managed to raise a smile because all he really wanted was Mum to be sitting with them.

"Och, she's been looking after us

boys for years," said Grandpa. "Time she had a life of her own, don't you think?"

Fergus wobbled a blob of jelly with his spoon. "Suppose," he said.

Grandpa nodded. "No suppose about it."

"Only . . ." Fergus began. "I just don't see why that life has to include Choppy Wallace. Why does Mum have to have HIM as a boyfriend?"

"Choppy?" Grandpa almost choked on a piece of pastry. "Choppy?" He coughed again. "Whatever gave you that idea?"

Fergus frowned. "But I thought –"

"You thought just because he'd been all smiles when he was round here your mammy'd fall for it?"

Fergus shrugged, but it was true, he did think that.

"Give the girl some credit, eh, sonny?" said Grandpa. "She just wanted to give him a chance, like we should always do with people."

"But he didn't deserve one," said Fergus.

"Maybe, maybe not," said Grandpa. "But anyway, it's not Choppy she's out with."

"Then who?" demanded Fergus. He racked his brains, trying to think of who would possibly be the best match for Mum. But there was only Dad. He really didn't want anyone else to be her fancy man. Unless . . . Fergus's heart flipped with possibility. There *was* someone he wouldn't mind as a stepdad. "Is it Steve 'Spokes' Sullivan?" he asked, hopefully.

"Did he secretly come to the race and see her in the crowd and fall instantly in love?"

Grandpa grinned and shook his head. "Sorry, sonny," he said. "It's not Spokes. Try a bit closer to home."

Closer to home? thought Fergus. "You mean Mr McGinty from number 20?" he said, worriedly. "But he's always in a bad mood and he doesn't believe in sweets and he hates dogs!"

At this, Chimp barked loudly as if in protest, although Fergus knew it was probably more because he was desperate for some steak.

Grandpa shook his head again. "Not Mr McGinty either! Try someone younger, someone kinder, someone who loves dogs, and sports, and cycling especially. Someone –"

"– with dark hair?" interrupted Fergus. "Who supports Hearts, and is always on our side and – and whose name rhymes with 'mambo'?"

Grandpa nodded. "Your mam," he said, "is out at Tony's Chinese for dinner, with none other than . . ."

"Jambo Patterson!" exclaimed Fergus. The funny thing was, he thought it would be weird saying it out loud, difficult, even. But it wasn't. It felt right and sounded right. Jambo was a great guy, after all, and he definitely believed in sweets, even if only as a treat, and he was almost never in a bad mood – well, only if Hearts lost to Hibs.

"You okay with that, then, sonny?" asked Grandpa.

Fergus nodded. "I guess I am," he said.

As he lay in bed that night, after Mum had got home and told him excitedly all about the meal, and given him a fortune cookie, Fergus thought about it again. He *was* all right with it. In fact he was *happy*. Seeing how happy Mum was had made him feel the same. His life may be wonky, but, like his birthday bike, it fit him just right.

"The only problem," he said, whispering to Chimp, who was on the floor with the fortune cookie in his jaws, "is going to be explaining it to Dad when he gets back, hey, boy?"

Chimp barked, letting the fortune cookie fall from his mouth and roll under the bed, a tiny sliver of paper fluttering out from it on the way. A sliver of paper that Mum would vacuum up the very next day before Fergus got to read the words printed on it in pale pink ink. "Your hope and courage could beat all the odds," it said.

But maybe Fergus didn't need to read it after all. Because, as he sunk into a deep, satisfied sleep, dreaming of the Nationals, and his dad on the doorstep welcoming the winners back home, his heart was filled with courage, and his head with hope. He *would* find a way to win, and a way to tell his mum and dad everything that had happened.

Which, he thought to himself in his dream, was an awful lot.

**Joanna Nadin** is the author of more than fifty books for children and teenagers, including the bestselling Rachel Riley Diaries and the award-winning Penny Dreadful series. Amongst other accolades she has been nominated for the Carnegie Medal and shortlisted for the Roald Dahl Funny Prize, and is the winner of the Fantastic Book Award, Highland Book Award and the Surrey Book Award. Joanna has been a journalist and adviser to the Prime Minister, and now teaches creative writing at Bath Spa University. She lives in Bath and loves to ride her rickety bicycle, but doesn't manage to go very fast. And she never, ever back-pedals . . .

Sir Chris Hoy MBE, won his first Olympic gold medal in Athens 2004. Four years later in Beijing he became the first Briton since 1908 to win three gold medals in a single Olympic Games. In 2012, Chris won two gold medals at his home Olympics in London, becoming Britain's most successful Olympian with six gold medals and one silver. Sir Chris also won eleven World titles and two Commonwealth Games gold medals. In December 2008, Chris was voted BBC Sports Personality of the Year, and he received a Knighthood in the 2009 New Year Honours List. Sir Chris retired as a professional competitive cyclist in early 2013; he still rides almost daily. He lives in Manchester with his wife and son.

The

series

Available now

The Best Birthday Bike

The Great Cycle Challenge

The Big Biscuit Bike Off

The Championship Cheats

and coming soon

The Winning Team

The Hercules' Hopefuls are going to the Nationals!
But will they be
THE WINNING TEAM?

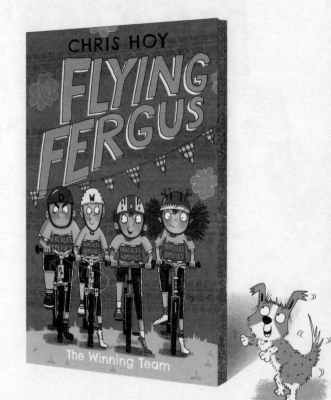

The stakes are high for Fergus and his friends
as they prepare for the National Championships
where they'll face their toughest opponents ever -
an all-girls super cycle team!

To discover more about
Fergus and his friends join
them at

FLYING
FERGUS
.com

There's loads to explore – learn more
about Chris Hoy, watch videos and get tips
and tricks for safe cycling and
taking care of your bike. You can
play games, solve puzzles and even
get exclusive sneak peeks of new
books in the series!

**JOIN
THE
GANG!**

Become a member of the fan club to keep up
to date with Fergus, Daisy and Chimp and be a
part of all their adventures. You'll have the chance
to build your own Flying Fergus character and
even choose your own bike to ride!